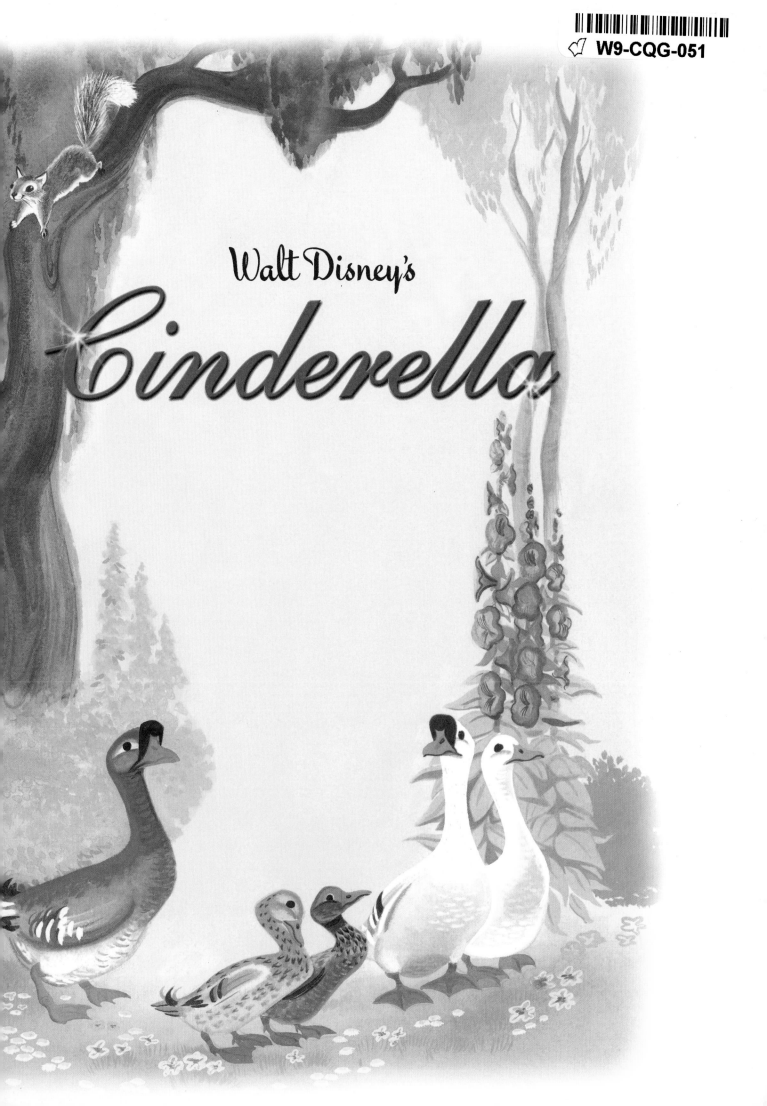

Walt Disney's
Cinderella

Senior Designer: Elaine Lopez
Editor: Sharon Yates
Editorial Director: Pamela Pia

Walt Disney's Cinderella copyright © 1950, 2001, 2004 Disney Enterprises, Inc.
Story adapted by Jane Werner. Illustrations adapted by Retta Scott Worcester.

CE

Walt Disney's

Cinderella

Illustrations by The Walt Disney Studios

Story adapted by Jane Werner

Illustrations adapted by
Retta Scott Worcester

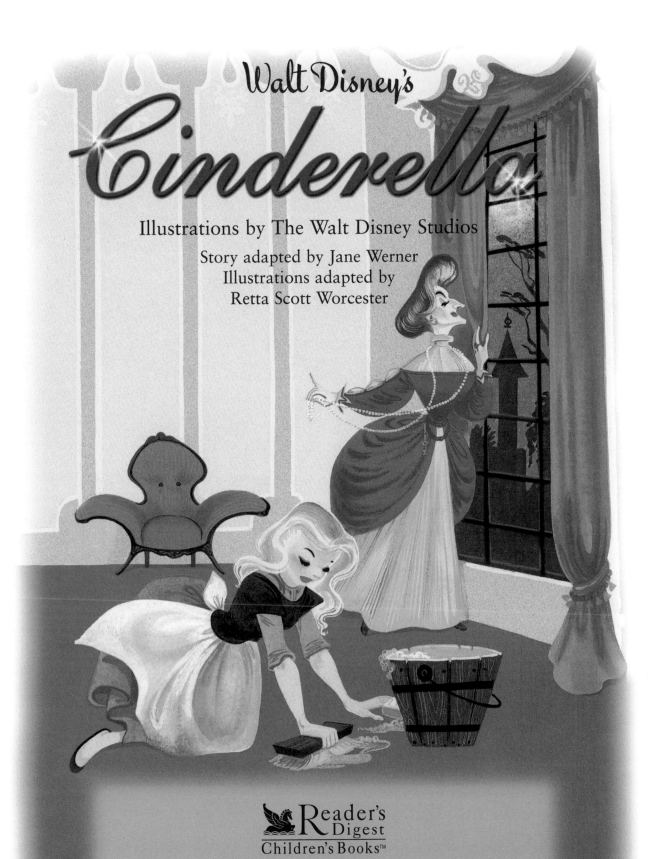

Reader's Digest
Children's Books™

Pleasantville, New York • Montréal, Québec • Bath, United Kingdom

Once upon a time in a far-off land, there lived a kindly gentleman. He had a fine home and a lovely little daughter, and he gave her all that money could buy — a pony of her own, a funny puppy dog, and beautiful dresses to wear.

But the little girl had no mother. She longed for a mother and for other children to play with. So her father married a woman with two daughters. Now, with a new mother and sisters, he thought his little daughter had everything to make her happy.

But, alas, the kindly gentleman soon died. His fine home fell into disrepair. And his second wife was harsh and cold. She cared only for her own two ugly daughters. To her lovely stepdaughter, she was cruel as cruel could be.

Everyone called the stepdaughter "Cinderella" now. For she had to work hard, she was dressed in rags, and she sat by the cinders to keep herself warm. Her horse grew old, locked up in the barn. And her dog was not allowed in the house.

But do you suppose Cinderella was sad? Not a bit! She made friends with the birds who flew to her windowsill. She became friends with the barnyard chickens and geese. And her best friends of all were — guess who? — the mice!

The musty old house was full of mice. Their homes were in the attic, where Cinderella lived. She made little clothes for them, and gave them all names. And they thought Cinderella was the sweetest, most beautiful girl in the world.

Every morning, Cinderella's friends the mice and birds woke her from her dreams. Then, it was breakfast time for the household — with Cinderella doing all the work, of course.

Out on the back steps she set a bowl of milk for the Stepmother's disagreeable cat, who watched for his chance to catch the mice. The faithful dog had a tasty bone. There was grain for the chickens and ducks and geese. And Cinderella gave some grain to the mice — when they were out of reach of the cat, of course. Then, back into the house she went.

Up the long stairway she carried breakfast trays for her
stepmother and her two lazy stepsisters. And down she came
with a basket of mending, some clothes to wash, and a long
list of jobs to do for the day.

"Now let me see," the Stepmother would say. "You can clean
the large carpet in the main hall. And wash all the windows,
upstairs and down. Scrub the terrace. Sweep the stairs — and
then you may rest."

"Oh," said Cinderella. "Yes." And off to work she went.

Now across the town from Cinderella's home was the palace of the King. And in the King's study one day sat the King himself, giving orders to the Grand Duke. "The Prince must marry!" exclaimed the King. "It is high time!"

"But, Your Majesty, what can we do?" asked the Grand Duke. "First, he must fall in love."

"We can arrange that," said the King. "We shall give a great ball, this very night, and invite every girl in the land!"

There was great excitement in Cinderella's home when the invitations to the King's ball arrived.

"How delightful!" the stepsisters said to each other. "We are going to the palace to a ball!"

"And I —" said Cinderella, "— I am invited, too!"

"Oh, you!" The stepsisters laughed.

"Yes, you!" mocked the Stepmother. "Of course you may go, if you finish your work," she said. "And if you have something to wear. I said *if*." And she smiled a horrid smile.

Cinderella worked as hard as she could, all the long day. But when it was time to leave for the ball, she had not a moment to fix herself up, or to give a thought to a dress.

"Why, Cinderella, you are not ready," said the Stepmother, when the coach was at the door.

"No, I am not going," said Cinderella sadly.

"Not going! Oh, what a shame!" the Stepmother said with her mocking smile. "But there will be other balls."

Poor Cinderella! She went to her room and sat down sadly, with her head in her hands.

But a twittering sound soon made her turn around. Her little friends had not forgotten her. They had been scampering and flying about, fixing a party dress for her.

"Oh, how lovely!" she cried. "I can't thank you enough," she told all the birds and the mice. She looked out the window. The coach was still there. So she started to dress for the ball.

"Wait!" cried Cinderella. "I am coming, too!"

She ran down the long stairway just as the Stepmother was giving her daughters some last commands. At the sound of Cinderella's voice, they all turned and stared.

"My beads!" cried one stepsister.

"And my ribbon!" cried the other, snatching off Cinderella's sash. "And those bows! You thief! Those are mine!"

So they pulled and they ripped and they tore at the dress, until Cinderella was in rags once more. And then they flounced off to the ball.

Poor Cinderella! She ran to the garden behind the house. And there, she sank down onto a low stone bench and wept as if her heart would break.

But soon she felt someone beside her. She looked up, and through her tears she saw a sweet-faced little woman. "Oh," said Cinderella. "Good evening. Who are you?"

"I am your fairy godmother," said the little woman. And from the thin air she pulled a magic wand. "Now dry your tears. You can't go to the ball looking like that!"

"Let's see now. The first thing you will need is — a pumpkin!" the Fairy Godmother said.

Cinderella did not understand, but she brought the pumpkin.

"And now for the magic words — *Bibbidi-Bobbidi-Boo!*" said the Fairy Godmother. Slowly, up reared the pumpkin on its pumpkin vine, and it turned into a handsome magic coach. "What we need next are some fine big — mice!"

Cinderella brought her friends the mice. And at the touch of the wand they turned into prancing horses.

Then the old horse became a fine coachman.

And Bruno, the dog, turned into a footman at the touch of the wand and a *Bibbidi-Bobbidi-Boo!*

"There," said the Fairy Godmother, "now hop in, child. You've no time to waste. The magic only lasts till midnight."

"But my dress —" Cinderella said, looking at her rags.

"Good heavens, child!" exclaimed the Fairy Godmother. "Of course you can't go in that! *Bibbidi-Bobbidi-Boo!*"

The wand waved again, and there Cinderella stood — in the most beautiful gown in the world, with tiny slippers of glass.

The Prince's ball was underway. The palace was ablaze with light. The ballroom gleamed with silks and jewels. And the Prince smiled and bowed, but still looked bored, as all the young ladies of the kingdom in turn curtsied before him.

Up above on a balcony stood the King and the Grand Duke, looking on. "Whatever is the matter with the Prince?" cried the King. "He doesn't seem to care for any of those beautiful maidens."

"I feared as much," said the Grand Duke with a sigh. "The Prince is not one to fall in love at first sight."

But at that very moment, he did! For just then, Cinderella appeared at the doorway of the ballroom. The Prince caught sight of her through the crowd. And like one in a dream, he walked to her side and offered her his arm.

Quickly, the King beckoned to the musicians, and they struck up a dreamy waltz. The Prince and Cinderella swirled across the dance floor. And the King, chuckling over the success of his plan to find a bride for the Prince, went happily off to bed.

All evening, the Prince was at Cinderella's side. They danced every dance. They ate supper together. And Cinderella had such a wonderful time that she quite forgot the Fairy Godmother's warning until the clock in the palace tower began to strike midnight. *Bong! Bong!*

"Oh!" cried Cinderella. The magic was about to end!

Without a word she ran from the ballroom, down the long palace hall, and out the door. One of her little glass slippers flew off, but she could not stop.

She leaped into her coach, and away they raced for home. But as they rounded the first corner, the clock finished its strokes. The spell was broken. And there in the street stood an old horse, a dog, and a girl in rags, staring at a small round pumpkin. Some mice ran chattering about them.

"Glass slipper!" the mice cried. "Glass slipper!"

And Cinderella looked down. Sure enough there was a glass slipper on the pavement.

"Oh, thank you, Godmother!" she said.

The next morning there was great excitement in the palace. The King was furious when he found out that the Grand Duke had let the beautiful girl slip away.

"All we could find was this one glass slipper," the Grand Duke admitted. "And now the Prince says he must marry the girl whom this slipper fits. He will not marry anyone else."

"He did?" cried the King. "He said he would marry her? Well then, find her! Scour the kingdom, and find that girl!"

All day and all night the Grand Duke and his servant traveled about the kingdom, trying to find a foot on which the glass slipper would fit. In the morning, his coach drove up in front of Cinderella's house.

The news of the search had run on ahead, and the Stepmother was busy rousing her ugly daughters and preparing them to greet the Grand Duke. For she was determined that one of them should wear the slipper and be the Prince's bride.

"The Prince's bride," whispered Cinderella. "I must dress, too. The Grand Duke must not find me like this."

Cinderella went off to her room to dress, humming a waltzing tune played at the ball the night before. Then the Stepmother suspected the truth: Cinderella was the girl that the Prince was seeking. So she followed Cinderella — to lock her in her room.

The mice chattered a warning, but Cinderella did not hear them. She was off in a world of dreams.

Then she heard the key click. The door was locked. "Please let me out — oh, please!" she cried. But the wicked Stepmother only laughed and went away.

"We will save you!" said the loyal mice. "We will somehow get that key!"

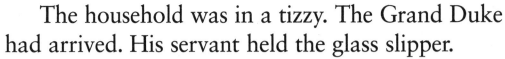

The household was in a tizzy. The Grand Duke had arrived. His servant held the glass slipper.

"It is mine! It is mine!" both stepsisters cried.

And each strained and pushed and tried to force her foot into the tiny glass slipper. But they failed.

Meanwhile, the mice made themselves into a long chain. The mouse at the end dropped down into the Stepmother's pocket. He popped up again with the key to Cinderella's room! At once, the mice hurried off with the key.

Now the Grand Duke was at the door, about to leave. Suddenly, Cinderella came flying down the stairs.

"Oh, wait, wait, please!" she called. "May I try the slipper on?"

"Of course," said the Grand Duke. And he called the servant back with the slipper. But the wicked Stepmother tripped the boy. The slipper fell and — *crash* — it splintered into a thousand pieces.

"Oh my, oh my!" said the Grand Duke. "What can I ever tell the King?"

"Never mind," said Cinderella. "I have the other one here." And she pulled the other glass slipper from her pocket!

So off to the palace went Cinderella in the King's own coach, with the happy Grand Duke by her side. The Prince was delighted to see her again. So was his father, the King. And so was everyone. For this sweet and beautiful girl won the hearts of all who met her.

Soon, she was Princess of the land. And she and her husband, the charming Prince, rode to their palace in a golden coach and lived happily ever after!